DARK CHOCOLATE

notionpress
.com

DARK CHOCOLATE

Rosetta

notionpress.com

Notion Press

Old No. 38, New No. 6

McNichols Road, Chetpet

Chennai - 600 031

First Published by Notion Press 2016

ISBN 978-93-5206-722-0

Foreword

Rosemary's journey has been one exhilarating ride. A melange of life and its shenanigans. Dark Chocolate attempts to bring to life this very journey. As the proof-reader and Editor of this wonderful short piece of literature, I inadvertently became a fellow traveller myself. Coasting through the waterfall of relationships and scrapping past their bruises. It's been one heck of an activity. My belief, that all of us would thoroughly enjoy this montage, is very strong.

Devraj Lahiri

Like the flower rose that comes with thorns and can bleed you if not handled with care, *Dark Chocolate* takes you through the nooks and corners of life that some might want to hide or forget, but here is a rose—Sheeba—that bares it for all. What does she achieve? Is it just redemption or does she hold the mirror where you get to see your real self?

Moumita Koyal (Madz)

Dark Chocolate is very close to me for a simple reason as I too play an integral part that I am aware of. Rose is a woman of substance, and she has opened her heart to write a part of her life which I think is phenomenal. Every woman is bound to be motivated by this story. She is the rose where her fragrance reaches everybody. I am happy to have had the opportunity to share the ups and downs with her. I wish her all the very best for her future endeavours!

Ruth Ann White (Jamie)

Preface

Relationships and their evolutionary crappiness are well-documented phenomena. History is witness to such eccentricity. And, trust me, no life is ordinary. They are all just different and weird in their own small utopia.

My attempt to bring forth the life I have lived in the past, the challenges I have at present and my eagerness to tear away into the future are well intended.

I have worn many hats. I have replaced the ones torn with new ones too. Being a fashion designer, I have been able to hold life at the corners to create an acceptable fit. Perfect I am not. Neither do I pretend to be one. I simply thrive in the imperfections of insanity.

I am insanity.

Acknowledgements

I would sincerely extend my acknowledgement to my lover, who always fills me with joy and has changed the way I look at the world! She has encouraged me to write this book!

Then there are other characters to whom I am very grateful. One of them is my bestie, whom I have tortured with all my drama, my half-sister Akira, who has been my silent listener, quite non-judgemental, my patient eleven-year-old daughter, a good-looking guy, who after I spoke to about my life, said it like a million times that an autobiography needs to be written. Last but not the least, another great guy, who is more than a friend, whom I wish I could marry, but I just don't see my husband in him, but a real support, so thank you! The best part is all these guys know who they are. So thank you for adding value to my life. Love all of you!

Introduction

Dark Chocolate is loaded with antioxidants that can positively affect your health! But hey, don't shut the book yet. This story is not about chocolates, but it is an autobiography of a woman whose life is a box filled with dark secrets, some secrets sweet and some dark—very dark secrets!

Let's call this character "Sheeba." Quite obviously she thinks she's a queen in the making! She is soaked in badassery, and she is a manipulative and self-obsessed bitch!

In her story, there are not too many characters—just a few men who ripped her soul apart, about two close gals who are her friends, her daughter and a lover who is also a girl! No, she isn't a lesbian by birth; yes, she falls in love with a girl! Ok, no time to freak out—read along. I promise you, this book will be unputdownable!

Chapter 1

One of the unexpected bonuses of divorce—which Sheeba realised when she settled down on her large comfy sofa with a glass of wine and a book of her favourite author—is that you become a sucker for romantic novels. Having the day of total quietness and extraordinary peace without the screaming of her eleven-year-old daughter, the only alive person with her is her pet, a handsome Labrador, whom she calls Hunter. Hunter was a priceless gift to Sheeba from her girlfriend, whom she calls "lover." Let's call Sheeba's girlfriend "Jamie." Jamie is a total animal lover whereas Sheeba is not, but she took an instant liking to Hunter—soon turning into blind love. She adored the little puppy a lot, and the puppy followed her around the house and treated Sheeba like a goddess.

Hunter's goddess was Jamie's too. She would often tell Sheeba, "You are my alpha and omega." The attention and the love she received from these two souls were all that mattered to her. Life was complete, or so she thought.

And yet, in spite of all the love that she was showered with, life was still a puzzle—a search—probably looking for a way to overcome the emptiness that she felt still lingered. Or was it just a mortal greed of wanting more? Sheeba did not have the answer, but it was the one she was frantically looking for.

Initially, when she separated from her husband six years ago, she was content, less jittery, less panicky and less cautious.

She was happy in the beginning, living her life, in a big house with huge windows and a spacious balcony, where she had placed a wrought iron sofa. The spot was her favourite haunt, where she smoked cheap branded cigarettes and Facebooked! The house was impressive but empty—much the way Sheeba felt about her life. Everything about the house shouted expense and never felt like home. She used to be happy having a husband and a child—hustling around the house—but they were gone! She rattled in the empty expanse growing more and more of being on her own—than she used to be.

Edward—her ex-husband—was a good-looking man, but Sheeba was never in love with him. They were married because she was afraid of being alone in the big bad world. So the first man—who loved and protected her—was married to on an impulse girl. She was all of twenty-two, naive and oblivious to the machinations of a marriage and surviving it. All she wanted was to be secure—both emotionally and financially. Ed did not even have a job then, but she did.

Love is all what you need—they say. However, an overdose of it can be unnerving too. Bordering obsessiveness, love can choke—a disconcerting feeling of asphyxiation leading to a sudden reactionary exercise of rebellious intent. Sheeba wanted to be liberated not because Ed wasn't a great husband or a fantastic dad—he was—but because both were not friendly. And the world beckoned her. Straight out of boarding, she jumped into the pitfalls of societal companionship for which she wasn't ready. The connivance of the world—trapping an individual in a web of customary and ritualistic orgy of daily mundane tasks—never suited her. She wanted her piece of pie and to enjoy it all by herself. Hence, by the time her daughter had turned four, Sheeba walked out of the marriage. Of course, the hurdles were all there, but she was bent upon overcoming them—hard hearted, yes, foolish, oh very much! She ran away.

Wasn't a very "Versace" act, she did agree. But circumstances did bring her back. The biggest being was her four-year-old daughter.

Life was never the same for her. She had become the centre of conflict, and the vacuum in her life pulled in even more turbulence. A new love had entered her life and she could not refuse it. There was nothing common between her and him, and it all started with that innocuous facade called friendship. The care, the small gifts and the comfort were followed by long walks, dinners and movies. Sheeba had also taught him to dress and speak well. His respect for her was immense, and it would soon turn into idolising. She was his friend, mentor and guide, and he her partner, protégé and lover. The small luxuries he could afford for her was now the world she so longed for.

Love and its many forms strike us at various stages of life. For Sheeba, it seemed relentless. She walked out of her marriage, again, to be with Mohsin. She loved the man and was willing to play by his rules. They managed to find a refuge in an apartment—garish by any standard. She was working in a multinational organisation and he was a salesman, with family responsibilities. The difference of their faith did not allow them to get married. But love did blossom. She would cook for him and wait for his return from work. The apartment soon turned into a home. There were adjustments too. He did not want her to work. She wore the clothes he wanted her to wear. Her choices of food changed too. The foodie was now more a dedicated lover than a gastronomist. Love is what Sheeba believed in, and that is what she was willing to live by.

She also turned out to be lucky for him. He prospered in his job and soon started out on his own. He would proudly admit it too—"Meri lucky charm."

But paradise soon darkened. Mohsin's visit to the house became more infrequent. The chasm between them—subdued all along—widened. The gifts and the dinners no more charmed her. His time was what she wanted, but time waited for none. Then, one day Sheeba who wanted to surprise him ended up at his shop, and the cookie crumbled. His sleazy ex was drinking juice with him. Now, Sheeba never had a problem with the juice, but cheating was not she would take lying down. He got the juiciest of slaps with an audience in tow, and she had made her point.

Sheeba went into a depression that later turned suicidal, after she had unearthed Mohsin's philandering ways. She was not the only woman in his life and there were many. Had it not been for Akira, her half-sister, Sheeba would have been dead for long—twice over. Sheeba's mother had remarried a Muslim, and Akira and two other sons were their children. Sheeba adored all of them, though the stepfather was not caring for her.

Akira and Sheeba are twelve years apart, but the chemistry they have is amazing. Along with Sheeba's eleven-year-old daughter, they turn the world into an insane trip, and it's worth riding it—a dream team setting the house on fire.

So coming back to Mohsin—the philanderer—who tried to make amends: Apologising on a dented relationship prolongs the pain though. They live together for a few more months, but things were never the same. She had to leave him—the better way to bail out than blackmailing a man into marriage—which Sheeba did in return for her abandoning a married life. He freaked out, got married within his community and escaped. Afterwards, Sheeba survived a painful few months and.

Songs—and importantly the meaning they try to portray—have reflected our own angst in many ways. Taylor Swift's *BlankSpace* was the one which Sheeba thought portrayed hers. For a moment, reminiscing about her lost love, while taking a swig of vodka, Sheeba knew that she has lived through those moments victoriously. The idea of "loving my man till I die" has now given way to a more independent and confident woman. The past has made her strong—both physically and emotionally. She has been cemented further by the presence of her daughter, who she adores. Sheeba is proud today to be a "great mother."

Her past had forced her to create a barrier around her—a wall. Her idea of a man had changed completely, and she wanted to keep it that way. She was a beast bludgeoning fate and smashing it to smithereens. Unstoppable is how she loves to describe herself.

However, broken after that incident, Sheeba was left to pick up the pieces of her shattered life. Isn't that how life testifies its presence, breaks itself and asks you to mend? But she did mend—a crazy diet with Pilates, weekend parties with loved ones, and a life of looking up. However, unemployment was irksome, which had to be fixed. As a warrior, Sheeba took a job with one of the country's finest fashion designers, learnt the trade, went solo and—three years later—was sitting back at her favourite sofa in the sweetest spot of her house—her balcony—sipping her favourite vodka. Life has come a full circle—content and satisfied.

A rose is visually stunning, but if holding it without much thought then the thorns will pierce you. Attitude and weak men do not gel. Sheeba is the rose she lives to think of.

Chapter 2

Well, Sheeba had her days when she was working for the multinational company. She worked hard and partied harder, but that was after she had mastered her responsibilities. Initially, she was the dumbest bitch of the lot—beauty with no brains. Her trainer hated her. She was married and was desperate to retain her job. Sheeba began to like him for his simplicity and wanted a way out of her marriage. She proposed him and was rebuffed and told of how his mother would not approve of the liaison and how unevolved the society was. She was taken aback and to this day has not been able to figure out what part does society play in one's personal life. As for the cute bong guy—the trainer-turned lover—he remained as caring and loving to her as ever. But husband he is not and probably will never be, for Sheeba does not see it that way anymore. Moreover, his mother and sister occupy the higher echelons of his feelings—something Sheeba finds unacceptable. She will never be the other love, but the only one—bad habit but that's how she is built. Sheeba knew him nearly for a decade and liked his company and friendship, but not as a lover and a husband—naah!

The reason Sheeba chose not to get married was probably because of the society shit—the trainer had thrown at her. "What a loser!" she thought of him who did not even have the courage to meet her at the cafeteria—a ball-less wonder and a sissy he. He could only console her when she got redeployed to another department. Much later, he did confess his disillusionment with society, but guess the ship had sailed by then.

But, every time when she is pissed with Jamie, she tells her she will marry him and settle down with him—bitchy Sheeba! After all, he was the only man she was comfortable with.

Work was difficult in the new department than in the previous one. It was scary too, more so with the new trainer—a woman—who had nil tolerance for stupidity and Sheeba. So every morning, after the frenetic madness of daily chores, Sheeba would head for her pickup and patiently wait for another day in hell. But soon she picked up the work and her trainer—Madz, the one mentioned earlier as the bestie—who became more of a friend. Madz had always judged Sheeba's arrogance as a colonial hangover—much like her surname. Later when she came to know of Sheeba's origin—a Bengali girl that Sheeba was—they paired to put the house on fire. Weekends meant parties and Mondays meant dark circles. Soul sisters they had become. It really warmed Sheeba, for she never actually had an elder sister, and being the eldest of the two, she had found someone to confide to.

There were hilarious incidents that interspersed their lovely friendship. Sheeba's over enthusiastic zeal to pronounce Lord Vishwakarma as someone from far Sheffield—"Veesh-waa-karmaa"—and then being told to shut up and stop being a foreigner and another one where she had gone to her manager for a sick leave only to be told that she was too decked up to even look remotely unwell where some which came to her immediately. Both were ludicrous happenings, and Madz and Sheeba still have a laugh thinking about them.

Sheeba would often cook dishes made of beef for the entire team, and they would all gorge on the food like hungry lions because eating beef in their houses were prohibited.

Madz was fiercely protective of Sheeba, and that would put off most guys because Sheeba was a natural charmer. She was not the typical beauty men so adore, but her ability to be friendly with everyone attracted a lot of attention—men mostly.

Sheeba had her frivolities. For a fashion show in office, she refused to walk with her male showstopper once for not being hot enough. Madz literally had to push her in, and since then the guy has not stopped chasing her. She knew her way to work around people—a natural instinct she was born with. Her many admirers were left heart broken when she left the organisation after three years—leaving behind an enviable legacy as a super performer, a friend to all and an individual of worth. It was a momentous year for Sheeba. She was a winner—both professionally and personally by having Mohsin in her life.

Of the many men who adored her, Sheeba loved just one. They worked together in the same team. He was a bong by birth, but all his mannerisms were like an English hip hop person—he would wear low waist jeans; he was a charmer with the girls who found him cute; and Sheeba and he were great friends. They would both crack non-veg jokes, which others did not understand. Work was fun because of him. He was the closest by example of a husband or a partner that Sheeba believed in—a pillar of strength. There were days Sheeba, he and a group of friends would hit the discos: Sheeba would be sloshed and he would come down like a thorough gentleman and hand over Sheeba to Edward who would wait outside in his press car.

They remained friends then and to this day they still are. He was the one who pushed her into penning this memoir. A super woman was what he would call her. Sheeba owed him a lot for her happiness. They both left at the same time: she to pursue her passion—clothes—and him, photography. The organisational work culture and structure had sapped them off their souls, and they felt trapped in a professional schism.

Madz and Sheeba lost touch once they parted professionally. But that was just an interlude. The friendship grew stronger once they met a few months later, and Madz's importance in Sheeba's life could be seen at the latter's first fashion show. Madz called the shots and that is how Sheeba wanted it to be. They would argue, fight and debate, but they did love from their hearts—isn't that's all to friendship?

Chapter 3

History—they say is a great teacher. The past with all its skirmishes is a lesson to look back to. Sheeba was born in a remote village. A place where women draped themselves in saris without blouses, and economy was still a far-fetched utilitarian term. You were either a hapless farmer or a spoilt zamindar. Sheeba's grandfather happened to be the latter. He had married two sisters—one of who was Sheeba's grandmother—because they both were beautiful. Her mother had married a Christian against Rajput traditions. Though the relationship between her mother and her grandparents was tenuous, it stuck on. Hell broke loose when Sheeba was born. The world—except her father—was against a girl child. Her grandparents disowned her mother, and Sheeba became the curse her mother never wanted.

As a result of this, the boarding school became her refuge. There was love—she so desperately yearned for—and respect—which she earned—and four-square meals. It was more of an orphanage, but for Sheeba, that was her world. She hated winter holidays, for that meant meeting her family who despised her. The hatred unnerved her. Her childhood felt robbed and being the eldest to six other kids meant more of babysitting than parenthood. Sheeba wanted to be a man for the woman in her who no more wanted to fight.

The memories of her boarding school light up her eyes. It's a faint tug that she feels in her heart. The serene calmness and the imposing yet beautiful church added to the peace of the surroundings. Her sadness and struggle would melt away somewhere within those confines. The huge playgrounds were surrounded by magnificent gardens. There would be long corridors connecting to the dormitories, and a long walk down that passage was like a meditation in motion. The thought of becoming a nun did cross her mind—something she laughs out to thinking about now.

Sheeba was never an outdoor girl, though she did play basketball and throw ball. Books and art and craft took away most of her time.

Thursday dinner meant beef curry. The only non-vegetarian day of the week, though Sheeba looked forward to all the days. Meals for breakfast would be two slices of bread and a glass of milk tea. Calling it a milk tea would be a misnomer. The vegetarian meals on the other days too were nutritious—a far cry from famished life she led at home. Sheeba could also ill afford the gifts other children would bring from their homes. She would use the discarded soaps and toothpastes after all had left for their holidays. She was too proud to ask for subsistence.

Sheeba was also proud of Shanaya—her only best friend in the boarding—her version of an angel. She would bring books, socks, toiletries and most of the necessities for Sheeba. Shanaya's dad would pack two neat packets of stuff labelling them with their respective names. Their friendship went beyond the walls of their beautiful school. So when Sheeba had her daughter, she named her Shanaya—a gratitude towards the friend who meant so much more than can be explained.

The adage "you can run but never hide" seemed so prophetic for Sheeba. Life does not give you the opportunity to hide—however far you have made your destination. School would never be an infinite affair, and Sheeba knew that she would have to return to the squalor eventually. She delayed it by another year by teaching street kids for five hours a day, getting paid four bucks an hour in the process. These were desperate measures, but she loved doing it. The kids eventually got admission into reputed schools, and she completed her company secretarial course—landing herself a job. The monthly salary was nothing to talk about, and her clothes to office were borrowed from the school charity. What was not borrowed was the urge to move ahead. Determined as she was, she did not give up.

A year later she moved into hospitality—front desk to be precise—with one of the India's finest hotel chains. She was also dating Edward then, who for a moment did provide her with a dilemma of choosing—him or the job. She stuck on with the job, and Edward with her. Her salary was barely sufficient, but her joys were unbound. She bought a bicycle for her baby brother with a part of her first salary, as she adores him. In fact it's the mutual love for each other that has survived the dark times. He also happens to be her business handler. Their discussions usually turn into arguments that, magically, turn back into fraternal love—strange are their ways. But love is strange.

And then Shanaya was born—the piece of her heart that fell from heaven. She gave up her job at the hotel to her sister—who was looking for one. Edward was working with a publishing house for a small stipend. However, Sheeba's world consisted only of her daughter—her manna from heaven. Her dream of getting married in a church never got fulfilled, and hence in Shanaya, she saw her fulfilment. She would already dream about the gown—the church full of folks—so Hollywood.

Two years passed and Sheeba was looking for a job. Expenses needed to be met, and she interviewed for the multinational company and cracked it. Sheeba got bored after four years down the line, which kick started her new role as a fashion designer. It is something she had dreamt of for a long time. She joined a fashion designer as a personal assistant—a stint that helped her hones her skills.

With the opening of her second outlet and the prospects of a third seemingly bright, Sheeba is today a woman in a rush. A happy soul with happy people is what her world is made of now—a world so different from the one that forced her to grow up so fast.

The relationship with her mother too had changed. They understand each other better now. The chasm has disappeared, and they now talk about everything under the sun.

Shanaya remains her fortitude—her support. They embrace like teenagers and giggle like long-lost friends. Mother and daughter are inseparable.

The weekdays of Shanaya are spent with her father and grandparents, but the weekends are for them together. Life becomes a bouquet of hope. Sheeba knows it and loves every bit of it.

Most of the weekends, Sheeba plans parties at her place. It's a habit Shanaya is not too fond of. She hates her mother boozing and smoking away to glory. Sheeba keeps promising her of kicking the habit. She knows she needs to. She also knows how difficult that would be. With Shanaya by her side, Sheeba really never needed any friends. Her circle of life seems to be complete. She has Hunter, her handsome Labrador, Jamie, her lover, and a fulfilled heart. There are occasional drop-ins by friends. The party just doesn't seem to stop. They all go into a depression once Shanaya leaves for her grandparents' home once the weekends end.

There are nights when Sheeba misses her sleep. Those are the days when she is on antidepressants and squirms in migraine. Those are the nights when Shanaya wraps her hand around her mother. That is the world Sheeba slowly dozes off it—lucky bitch. The once lonely woman now has a complete universe for herself.

Sheeba does not hide anything from Shanaya. She has been very upfront about her relationship with Mohsin and the reasons behind her acrimony with Edward. She also asked for forgiveness from Edward, but he did not relent. Shanaya had asked her mother to live her life her own way the way she was. Sheeba was a great mother, and Shanaya loved her for what she was.

However, there is an uncomfortable truth that keeps haunting Sheeba—her relationship with Jamie. Shanaya knows them to be great friends, but lovers that they are is something Sheeba would want her know—afraid of being judged by a person she would give up the world for.

Chapter 4

Patience is a virtue mankind is so confused with, and it was something Sheeba was not too fond of. She wanted the world to have a sneak into her inner world. A world she had lost years back and was now waiting for that miracle to lighten it. Sheeba was never worried about the brickbats or the darkness it involved. She had lost her innocence long time back. All she wanted now was to inspire. She also wanted to love, hold hands, sing and dance in the rain and go on for long unplanned adventures.

And Jamie came into her life.

The first date Sheeba and Jamie went out for was spent sitting at different tables with the daughter and nephew, respectively. They weren't even facing each other, except the texting that connected them. They were too scared to tell the kids. The real conversation started after they went back home. Night gradually descended into day as the cell phone and Skype—modern man's creation—destroyed distance, and love blossomed.

To think of it, all of this started with a dare. Her friends challenged her to kiss a lesbian, and the daring bitch—that she is—accepted it. Sheeba found Jamie—an attractive, tomboyish woman on the net—and seduced her. She also discovered Jamie to be her junior in school—a naughty brat. Jamie too fell for her. She was the best looking lesbian Sheeba did find for herself. Jamie was fair with spiked hair and a cute smile.

She was shorter than Sheeba, which Jamie always wanted to make up for. Sheeba's love—at a later stage—was unconditional, and she loved Jamie just the way she was.

Sheeba decided to meet a month later and that did happen after a lot of coaxing. She also had to be truthful about her real identity on which Jamie had hung up the phone. Moments later, she called back and professed her love for Sheeba.

Love is blind. Let's add insanity to it. Suddenly, the extreme homophobe—that Sheeba was—would now eagerly wait for Orange is the new Black. No gender, no race and no caste—it's just madness unbound. It's an everlasting conversation that would last for the next two years.

Experiences change an individual. Fears turn into passion, the inhibition of needles into craze for tattoos, fear of dogs into love for Hunter and vertigo into airplane rides. Life is all about acquiring new tastes and turning new pages. It is so much more than the craze for coitus, and it's more basic—emotional. Sheeba found Jamie and now she had the world at her feet.

Similar to mirage, the horizon slowly faded.

Two years into the relationship, the ship slowly but surely began to toss around. Choppy waters—Sheeba would not blame Jamie for everything though. She was in touch with Mohsin—more out of responsibility as a mentor—for the love was no more there. This upset Jamie who would not allow any man or woman near her lover. They were partners forever, and Jamie would not have anything other than that. Sheeba would work outdoors, and Jamie would work from home. This would also allow Jamie to stalk Sheeba that annoyed her infinitely.

A point did come when Sheeba wanted to move on. She wanted peace in her life, but Jamie was a habit now—a love she could not reconcile with nor throw away. Jamie also knew of all of Sheeba's secrets—something she regrets of sharing to this day. Jamie would throw these at her face after fight. It was getting unpleasant for Sheeba. Jamie had also called the cops charging Sheeba of stealing. It was a sin. Sheeba would rather die than steal. She has forgiven Jamie for this, but she would never forget. She knew Jamie did all this to get her back. The method was incorrect, but the intention wasn't.

Sheeba wanted to rewind and correct her mistakes, but time lost is forever gone. However, Sheeba—the sucker for love—would succumb to Jamie's relentless love despite the quarrels, the hurting taunts and the emotional scars.

Love is blind indeed.

Not many would have the courage to stand up to Edward—Sheeba's husband, a 6 feet 3 inch of pure muscle—but Jamie would. She would literally mock him of how his wife was now her lover and that he could do shit. But he wasn't the only one on the wrong side of Jamie. Mohsin—the cute bong—and innumerable other men who had a thing for Sheeba would be warded off. Till a point, even Sheeba thought Jamie as her world. However, when love becomes suffocating and you start asphyxiating for the want of release, it's time you move on. Sheeba thought the same.

Jamie was psychotic—eccentric to the point of perversion—an extreme form of contradiction that could harm. She could love like hell but could equally adept at hurting—highly opinionated, unpredictable and abusive when drunk. She was also a dreamer, but not always a doer. She was definitely the sexiest but physical beauty dulls if you are oppressive.

Sheeba was also a contradiction—a characteristic that she imbibed while in the relationship. Every time, when they broke off, Jamie would hook up with another girl and Sheeba would retaliate. She wanted Jamie back in her life.

Love is funny.

Jamie was a loyal lover. Sheeba would make fake profiles to check on her partner. She would flirt with her like the old days—expecting Jamie to flirt back. But the lady was forthright about her relationship to anyone who wanted to talk to her. This made Sheeba fall for her more. It was love for Sheeba, but Jamie was an obsessive lover; obsession throttles love. It becomes more of subjugation.

Sheeba knew she had to get out, and her in-laws helped her out. She also put up a restraining order for Jamie and hooked up with Andrew, her childhood lover—a loser then and even now. All this happened to put an end to Jamie. After four years, they madly fell in love with each other.

Chapter 5

Andrew came to Sheeba's life at a time when she was all of thirteen.

Andrew was a striking, handsome, rugged and athletic young man then. In a small town of Anglo-Indians, he is the only boy worth drooling for and every girl did just that. But for him, Sheeba was the one. Now our girl was not a pretty lady in the natural course of things, but what made her attractive was her persona and the intelligence to boot. They dated till she was nineteen before Andrew's mother and Andrew's philandering ways broke it off. The girl—Andrew cheated on Sheeba for—was later to be his wife and the mother of two beautiful daughters.

Before they broke off, the love birds would meet in the park and the basketball court in Andrew's hostel—during his matches—where she would cheer him like a hysterical schoolgirl.

Sheeba would help Andrew morally and emotionally at times, for he was studying at that time. Those were the days when cell phones never existed. Therefore, they would call each other at designated numbers in pre-decided places, but Andrew was never available. Sheeba would visit his hostel, and he would send his cousin to lie till one day the cousin told Sheeba that Andrew was simply not interested in her—that was her first break-up. However, they still remain friends to this day. That was the first time of the numerous times that

Sheeba went into men-related depression. Later she discovered that Andrew had been seeing someone else and just did not have the heart to break hers—loser!

So after a decade when he flown down to Kolkata, they met and sparks did fly. The story probably had never ended. They pick up from where it had ended. Andrew was a shadow of his former self—bald and pot-bellied. Sheeba was a striking vixen now. She had discussed Jamie with Andrew and wanted him to move in with her—which he did. However, love was the last thing Sheeba wanted at this moment. She wanted someone who would listen to her and understand life—not as an extension of existence but as a fulfilment. It started off well. They spoke of yesteryears and giggled like teenagers. They talked about embarrassing moments—like the one when Andrew had seen Sheeba off on the wrong train, she panicked and jumped off the running train. They all laugh now reminiscing those days.

Sheeba liked Andrew because he would crack her up. Laughter they say is the greatest uniter. He was also a criticizing oaf—always at Sheeba's back about the changes that has happened to her which he disapproved off. Sheeba would only murmur "too bad" under her breath—that was the Sheeba who was long gone. This was the reincarnation—anew, fabulous, strong Sheeba!

She was constantly on the lookout for a soul mate, who would also be a realistic and pragmatic individual—brutally honest. She was done with the "I Love You Forever" syndrome. They had discussed this once, but that was before Sheeba had gulped down an entire bottle of wine and passed out.

When she woke up, drooling over his strong arms, Jamie was the first face that came to her mind. That was also the first she prepared breakfast for a partner. Jamie would not let her do it. She would insist to be her butler for life and the chef at large. Sheeba would occasionally cook for her, or it was just coffee at times.

Andrew kept staring back her throughout breakfast with a wicked smirk. He confessed that he had never seen this side of Sheeba and he was quite perplexed. He loved it though.

One day Sheeba skipped work—pillow fights, scrabbles and catching up on the days gone by were all they did.

Andrew did regret leaving Sheeba and wanted her back by his own terms and conditions, but the bitch had moved on.

Sheeba got married to Edward before Andrew did and went on to live right next to him—vengeful for being cheated. But those were all from the past. Much water had flown beneath most bridges of life, and they both were now individuals with a hold on themselves.

When Andrew walked in, she did not have much hope on the relationship, though somewhere in the corner of her heart did she want it to work. He was smart, witty and level headed. But he was someone who would take advantages too. Sheeba was being used again, and she saw through it.

The tipping point came one day when Sheeba had requested him to put her legs on his lap and press it, so that the cramps she usually got would go away. Only to be told by him that it would be degrading for him to touch a woman's foot. However, "using a woman was not one!!!"—hypocrite.

They started in January, Sheeba's birthday, and it ended in November, his birthday. She calls it a "Sweet n Sour November."

Solitude is mirage a life provides you with to fool you. One moment you have it and poof—it's gone.

It's very much like being in a relationship. You think things are fine when suddenly they change, and all you can do is wonder what hit you.

Was Andrew a boon or a bane? He was probably both. But at least this time Sheeba did not have her heart involved.

Life does give you chances, but we are either too blind to see it or too preoccupied and let it go. Love can wait at times. Sheeba now needed a focus—on her blooming career, family and, more importantly, herself. It's too much of a struggle to stay in love. Making a life is a much easier proposition.

Nothing slips out of your hand if you are sincere. Probably she let Andrew slip because she knew he was not the one.

Chapter 6

One could be easily mistaken now that was the end of the road of Sheeba. Another relationship blundered—another new bout of depression. But it could not be farther away from the truth. It was a new start. What had actually made her stronger was her departure from Jamie. Jamie was a pillar Sheeba held onto—a partner who would never give up on her. However, Jamie was also an uncontrollable maniac. When mixing her with alcohol, it will all be brimstone and fire. They would end up biting and scratching each other. The hurt would go much deeper. The flesh smoothens, but the scar remains. The last time they spat—usually what these two girls would do—it was the final time. Cops had to be called and the only people who steadfastly supported Sheeba were her in-laws. She remains indebted to them. It was a misunderstanding that caused all this. Sheeba's business was not going well and the finances were shaky, so she got into a partnership with her younger brother, instead of Jamie, as promised. Jamie misconstrued it while all Sheeba wanted was for Jamie to start her own business first. The madness that ensued even got Hunter worried and he would constantly guard Sheeba from any harm. Sheeba—the proud lady that she was—could no more remain deaf to Jamie's abuses and left in the middle of the night.

The note she left for Jamie:

13th of June cannot be scarier than this, Jamie.

I am leaving you forever, for the future I had dreamt with you is no more happening.

You are not the same person under alcohol.

I begged you to stop abusing and hitting me last night, but you would not listen.

I am leaving Hunter and Shanaya too.

No man can give me the happiness that you have given me, but I am also tired of looking over my shoulder like forever.

You have taught me love but also to hate. I always don't wish to be careful. I wanted to be liberated. That was the very reason I split up with Edward.

Don't worry about me. I will be just fine.

Sheeba

Jamie was furious. She smashed the television and threatened to burn the house down. But for Sheeba, she had enough.

Sheeba went to the airport and roamed aimlessly before deciding to go over to her hometown, where she stayed in a lodge. She went back to her mother's place and locked herself up for four days. She was not moving in with Jamie. It was more fear than anger.

The past never leaves you though. It festers as an unscratched itch—a wound that bleeds. You can bandage it with frivolities, but the pain sticks. Still you gather courage to rip it open and crush the core.

Sheeba was a free bird now—off commitments, relationships and heartbreaks. She had recently been through the opening of her second boutique and was firming up plans for a third. Hunter was her shadow, and Shanaya her wall. However, the void remained and she could feel it. Therefore, she walked up to Jamie, after all the bickering, and commanded her to come back. Jamie sheepishly followed her back. But, this time around Jamie had turned into the quintessential supervisor, for Sheeba had a dead worm in her brains that needed to be calcified. Adding to it the bouts of depression and the nagging migraine, Sheeba was a health wreck and Jamie was the nightingale looking after them—Hunter included. All the bitterness had long vanished but so did the love. They were long-lost friends now holding each other in times of need. But the distance had grown. The mushy emoticons had changed to smileys and thumbs up. Maybe, they had given everything they had to give each other to an extent that all they now had was blankness. They were still soulmates, but the estrangement of their souls was evident. They loved each other's company, but probably the hearts wished to stay apart.

Jamie was less into booze now. It was very good, but she was even lesser into Sheeba, which bothered her. Jamie was still the passionate woman willing to help someone with the last penny she had. But love—that's a bird poets romanticize—had flown.

Jamie had struggles with her identity right from the beginning. The reason why Sheeba was so very loved by her was because she embraced Jamie as who she was. She accepted her in her totality, although she was still a morbid homophobe. But Sheeba goofed up when Edward had asked her about Jamie. She regrets it to this date. However, all that was in the past. Sheeba was no longer the village belle but the fiery urban chic—the society has damned.

The world's been quite interested about Sheeba's preferences, and she's been hounded about it too. But patience is not an infinite tool. It does wear away.

Sheeba has had her share of temptations, but she had also come to realise the sacrifices Jamie had made for her. That is the reason why the world slowly became an uninteresting place for her. Jamie was all she wanted—got and had. Though the love might not be all that evident now, the bond remains. And how? Jamie had her share of fun during the break-up period, but she too was a loner. The human soul craves.

Sheeba remembers the first time they had planned a holiday—Darjeeling, where they wanted to settle down forever. The locals would call Jamie "Sir" and prohibit her to use the ladies washroom.

The second vacation was at Goa—sun, sand and booty. That vacation was a crazy one—shining hotels, drugs, dancing on table tops and singing in the middle of the beach. It was a life both yearned for.

Jamie—though younger—was the protective one. She would protect Sheeba like a bear hug. Suitors—and there were plenty—were frightened by the sight of her.

For Jamie, Sheeba was the queen. She would not allow her to get distracted by household chores. Jamie would take care of all that. Sheeba would be focusing solely on her business. Jamie was also very fond of Shanaya. She would take care of her during her weekend visits. Shanaya knew about their fights, but she too was very fond of Jamie and would tell her how much her mother loved her. For Shanaya, they were just friends though. Sheeba at times would feel guilty about the way she would use Jamie. Probably, Jamie sensed that too. However, love made you do incredible thing, and their relationship was an example of it.

Every time when Sheeba would try to get close to Jamie, the past would rear its ugly head up—more acrimony, more bickering, more people and cops. Love has a way with things. It enamours; it hurts too—awfully.

Blood too flowed, bruised hands and battered heads—but it all seemed to be perfectly set puzzles in their imperfect jigsaws. Love lorded all.

They broke up ten times in four years and made up each time. They were friends first. They would share their sorrows and their happiness. They would laugh, cry and booze. They just could not keep each other away. They couldn't keep each other together though.

Jamie always wanted a kid from Sheeba—of course from a donor. Sheeba would baulk at the idea. Jamie wanted a family to return to every evening.

Sheeba—the ever committed homophobe—just could not reconcile with the idea of partnering Jamie—in spite of all the love. She prays for a person who will. Jamie needs someone.

Life is one helluva rollercoaster, and Sheeba's been riding well, hoping the distance gets covered quickly.

Chapter 7

Some great guy has written this keeping a woman in mind—salute you:

She doesn't need expensive gifts. She doesn't need expensive dinners. I mean sure of all those things would be nice, but all she really needs is you. She needs your listening ear when she is ready to vent. She needs your shoulder to cry on when life gets hard on her. She needs your words of encouragement when she is getting ready to pursue her dreams. He needs to feel safe around you and know that you have her best interest when it comes to her heart. And if it's taking a while to take you in, she is trying to punish you. She just doesn't want to repeat making the same mistakes she has made in the past of giving a man her all—just to find out that he couldn't match her effort. Love her genuinely. Love her patiently. Love her passionately. And last—but not the least—love her consistently, and in return, she will love you like you have never been loved before.

And this is where Jamie failed miserably.

There was a time when Jamie would shower Sheeba with the most expensive stuff. But now she can't afford and Sheeba knows it. However, she never wanted those gifts in the first place. All she craved for was a partner who would listen to her rants—a shoulder to place her soul on. She never wanted the riches. She never ever ran after money. She wanted love. Jamie had taught her to love, but Jamie was too temperamental—a heady mix of mood swings and alcohol. Lately, Jamie had grown lethargic too. She seemed to be uninterested in the world around. The early morning coffee and the household chores that Jamie would do with such flourish—all of that would be in the past. The love and care was certainly gone.

There would be arguments, and the subject of the argument would vary—Hunter's diet, window curtains, television, anything and everything.

Sheeba would rush through her manuscript while Jamie would watch TV—at the lowest volume. And Jamie wouldn't be too happy about it. Sarcastically she would ask Sheeba, whether the TV needed to be shut off. Gritting her teeth, Sheeba would slowly close her laptop and go off to sleep.

She did wonder at times—why could not her dream be somebody else's too?

Mornings are manic. The rush is palpable. She needs to be rushing off to her boutique. She also has her workshop attached to it. Her tailors work away furiously as Sheeba—the business woman—takes over. She loves her job—lives and breathes it. She also loves her solitude. Close to her workshop is her hideout—a cosy 200-square-feet den. It has an attached kitchen, a washroom and a chandelier. It also has a huge mirror. A small couch and a desk complete it. Drawing the gold-rimmed curtains, putting the air condition on, Sheeba would immerse herself in her story.

She was never the petite belle nor the fairness type, but Sheeba was the glam doll—the hot chic types.

Someday she would wear her torn jeans and a singlet and strut out like a peacock. The world would crash around. Sheeba knew how people would ogle at her, but the queen bee was too damned about it. Her confidence reflected in her dealings with her clients too—not one could escape her selling power.

At times she would re-imagine her old clothes, which would be cutting and sewing them back as something new. Making clothes for Shanaya was also her favourite. The size of the order did not really matter, as the soul that went into it did.

The other world Sheeba loved living in was her workshop. Amidst the fabrics, her sewing machines and her tailors, Sheeba would romanticize life. There would be discussions about family, clothes and fate in general. Her favourite—whom she would lovingly called "Chotu"—would often be argumentative. But, they were all in awe and respect of their boss. Sheeba is a people's leader, and her workers would fear her as much as adore her. Her daily routine would include morning discussions, outdoor consultations and copious amount of tea. The adrenaline needed to flow.

All this—though still at a nascent stage—never came easy to her. All she started with was a sewing machine and a tailor. Home was her workplace and she would deliver her products to her clients. Over a period of time, a small place was rented and people started visiting her, and by the third year, a small store came into existence. She hopes to open a bigger store next year exclusively for wedding gowns as she never got to wear one. She wanted to sew many for others. Some dreams take you to places—Sheeba's dream created one for her.

Three years into her business, Sheeba has learnt the art of tact. She knows her way into and around dealings, and it has kept her in good stead. Along the way, she has also made some close friends. Ritisha—for example—is a sweet bubbly and energetic girl who also happened to be one of Sheeba's early customers. They would go out for girls' parties, swimming and shopping. Sheeba—being the elder one—is also Ritisha's resident adviser. She had other friends of her age but always finds solace in Sheeba's company. Ritisha would share all her secrets with her. Sheeba's world was a very close knit one—

Jamie, her lover, Hunter, her shadow, Shanaya, her angel, Madz, her bestie, Akira, her half-sister and partner in crime, and now Ritisha. With such a fascinating universe to orbit in, our queen bee really never found any interest elsewhere.

Akira and Ritisha were in awe of Sheeba. They would admire her zest for life—the can-do attitude. They would also go gaga over Sheeba's sexiness, for which Sheeba would blush and deep within a sense of pride will suddenly soar up. It was because many years before Sheeba turned out to be a swan, she was a gawky teenager—bespectacled, long wild hair and without an iota of imagination in her dressing sense. The big bunny teeth were the most predominant feature her maxi facial inherited. However, transformation in an individual's life happens at various times. Hers happened at the age of thirty—and lo and behold. She changed into an enamouring bitch; men couldn't keep their eyes off. It was quite a change literally. The lady had grown unbounded—both physically and mentally. Guess… experience did play a very big part in it—life, as they call it.

Akira and Sheeba—despite having different fathers—were the two inseparable sisters. The former would be amazed how Sheeba closely knit her world and that she was loved by everyone. To this Sheeba would wryly smile and say, "Just falls into place."

They talk about everything. Jamie does come up for discussion and Sheeba keeps telling her how disappointed she is with the relationship and intends to break up. Next morning, it all changes though. Before Shanaya was born, Sheeba was the mother to her three half-brothers and half-sisters, which was very much evident.

Akira and Jamie were on good talking terms. They were part of the girl gang who would paint the town red. Jamie was very fond of Akira. She would keep telling her how she reminded her of her younger sister. Jamie had won over Sheeba's family and was loved by all unlike Sheeba who was the most hated in Jamie's family. This did not bother her though. She knew as long as Jamie loved her she was alright. Sheeba was no sugar-coated candy. She was a hard nut and loved the way she was. Jamie let Sheeba be her way and that is the reason why she stuck on with her for the longest time.

Chapter 8

Sheeba wanted her own space—her own bubble. But she would not also want to be ignored. Jamie had become busy with her life. There was a time when Jamie would call her up incessantly and now it's just thrice in a week, and that too mostly work related or for Hunter. Sheeba was back to her solitude and work. Empire building needed focus and guts, and Sheeba intended to use both vigorously.

Life with all its frivolities causes upheavals in one's life in a manner that trying to manage it costs you your entire life. Controlling it is impossible. Similarly, trying to hold onto someone who is not as worth as holding onto has the same dilemma, nor if someone was to run away for fear of getting hurt. These were existentialist stress points one lives with throughout his or her life.

Strength is inherent. Sheeba wanted someone with bigger hearts—longer anchors. She needed someone who had no qualms about the world judging them. They would follow their emotions and build a world around it.

Probably both wavered at their intentions. Jamie wanted to have kids—a family. She wanted to share her name with Sheeba. And for Sheeba, no matter how much she loved Jamie commitment was the last thing she could ever bring upon herself. She just could not trust herself. She suffered from the delusion of failure that she was not good enough for a relationship.

Sheeba's wants were more superficial. Loving her, being there with and for her, making coffee for her and staying awake as long the insomniac did were some of her wants. She was not the disloyal one. But neither did she really approve of a relationship that clinged on to the hopeless vestiges of commitment. Her relationships were expected to be breezier and less hang-ups. She was proud of Jamie and their same-sex relationship. But commitment…?

Jamie's dad was diagnosed with terminal mouth cancer. She was spending more time with him—nursing him. And one day, somebody over a conversation mentioned cheating to Sheeba. And then the idea percolated into her hyper-charged brain and Sheeba turned into a lost cause. The bipolar that she was, Sheeba's case worsened. She trusted Jamie from the bottom of her heart, but a suspicion seeped deep within is like cancer and spreads like wildfire out of control. During their fights, Sheeba would thrust these questions of cheating on Jamie's face. It was with equal fervour—denied. She had also stalked Jamie on social forums. Sheeba was a possessive woman, and nobody could eye Jamie—nobody!

Karma they see is a bitch. It travels in circles and it did for Sheeba. Finally, Jamie did open up about her feelings to Sheeba:"I have loved you Sheeba and put you on a pedestal, in spite of all your shortcomings. I have been committed to you, given you my all, and all you did was treated me like door mat, and I still waited like a fool. You seem to enjoy your freedom if that makes you happy; I am willing to give that to you, on a condition, 'you must be happy'. I see you have a bright future—we both must move on!"

That was the heaviest weight Sheeba had ever carried. It choked her.

There was not a single word that Sheeba could think of saying. Probably, she did not want to. They both loved each other. But the togetherness was lost. Sheeba had built a wall around her, but the emotions were too strong to resist. She wanted to protect herself from breaking down after numerous soul-ripping experiences. Hence, she could never fully open up to Jamie, and that came back home to roost. She dragged herself to agree with Jamie. She did not want to spoil her young lover's life by blocking her life. Jamie still had so much to live for—so much to experience.

Every time when she would want to get off Jamie, the memories would flood her thoughts. She would reminisce how dream like their relationship was. The four o'clock coffee, the drool over arms, the cuddle and the kiss—yes, Jamie was the best kisser Sheeba had ever come across. She knew how to keep her woman happy in bed. Jamie was a magnet Sheeba could never resist, and they were fire in a waterfall—fluid yet concurrent, flowing on their own, never to mix and unstoppable. Sheeba did try to get intimate with other men after they ended their relationship, but no one could satisfy her. Edward would suggest that she had now become a total lesbian, but Sheeba knew it was not the gender but the individual that mattered. Jamie was pure heaven. The rest seemed so mortal.

Before Jamie had come into her life, Sheeba has been through a few relationships. None of them were anything to write home about. Jamie's arrival had changed all that. Jamie was a package. She was an arrogant woman—a big mouth. However, she was who she was and Sheeba loved every bit of her.

Jamie would come up with weird stuff to irritate Sheeba, when the latter was down. She would pick her nose just to make her lover freak who incidentally was a cleanliness freak. Jamie would also deliberately misspell and mispronounce things. These were not much, if you look at from afar, but they all added to something so lovely. Life is indeed made up of such extremely tiny moments. These are what we live for.

Sheeba was in a dilemma. The ball was in her court. She had one door to freedom wide open, but it also did lead to loneliness. She would wake up—thinking about all these—in the middle of the night. Hunter would get a sense of it. He would slowly come over and place his head on her lap. Dogs are nature's best gift in solitude. They will nurture you. In the morning, Hunter would wet Sheeba's face. And if she still wouldn't wake up, he would pull the blanket off. He was Sheeba's foolproof alarm. He was also the unconditional love Sheeba had in an otherwise empty life.

Hunter was also one of the main reasons why Sheeba did not want to let go of Jamie. She was his papa and Hunter loved his papa as much as he loved her mom. Jamie too was extremely fond of Hunter. Although Hunter had Shanaya during the weekends, it was papa he would look out for.

It was tough for Jamie. She was leaving two of her most loved ones, but she had to. It wasn't a sudden decision for her and nor she was doing anything wrong. She was simply safeguarding her feelings. Sheeba too was stuck within her own walls. She too wanted Jamie to move on, for she herself was unable to move ahead. They both were still friends—soulmates. However, the love had seemingly disappeared somewhere. Both pairs of eyes would fleetingly search for it, but suddenly even the horizon looked so far off.

Chapter 9

There's a final secret that needs to be told. The cupboard would then seem to be clean. You see—in journey—and meet a lot of people: most leave but some stay. This too is a journey. Let's just say, Sheeba wanted all of us to undertake it along with her, and here's her secret.

Remember, we spoke about a sweet bong chap—someone who worked with Sheeba during her stint at the multinational organisation. Now, he was a nice guy whom Sheeba liked a lot. In fact, today whatever she is as a successful businesswoman should be credited to Abhishek. So now we name him as one—Abhishek. They've known each other for nine years, and the friendship still stays. Abhishek is a great guy who suffers from overconfidence at times. He is no looker who thinks no end of himself, but he is a cute teddy bear you'd want to hug—not being a Brad Pitt ideally does not make a man bad. Abhishek has been a great support to Sheeba throughout her formative years. At the beginning of their friendship, Sheeba did toy with the idea of getting married to him. Those were the days, when our lady was a rather Plain Jane—no parties, no boozing and no smoking. She is a simple catholic girl who would work tirelessly and enjoy Abhishek's company. But, Abhishek's mother did play the spoilsport—this is how he put it—saying his mother would freak out at their idea of being married. Abhishek too was rather timid about the idea of getting married to someone outside his religion. Society and mother proved to be too overbearing for him.

Jamie and Abhishek are both Librans—balanced and nuanced in their approach to life—and both were very loyal to Sheeba.

After a point, Abhishek was getting tired of providing a shoulder to Sheeba after every fight with Jamie. He popped the question of marriage to Sheeba which was very succinctly put down by Sheeba. She was no more ready to get married to anyone, but Abhishek would remain her close one forever. Jamie and Abhishek knew about one another. The world was indeed a very small place to live in.

Over a period of time, Abhishek had learnt to be patient with Sheeba. He has slowly been able to adapt himself to Sheeba's wants.

Sheeba and Abhishek would go on short vacations. He would take her to the most expensive places and shower her with the most expensive gifts. He loved it though such fancies had no meaning for Sheeba. She just adored his company. Sheeba trusted Abhishek and relied on him for everything. Sheeba trusted him to that extent where she signed a blank cheque and gave it to him and said, "Someday when I become a millionaire you are allowed to take out how much ever you want." Abhishek looked at the cheque lovingly and put it away in his pocket. Sheeba could blindly trust him, and he never disappointed. Sheeba worked very hard at her business, but no doubt without his undeniable help she wouldn't have reached where she is now.

Abhishek is a wealthy man, but he also knew the value of money as he started from scratch. He was a poor guy then who followed his dreams and realised them to respect! However, his weakness remains Sheeba and knows no bounds while spending on her. His intention is similar to that of Jamie though—Sheeba's happiness.

Today whatever Sheeba has achieved has been because of the support of Abhishek. He has been selfless in his friendship with her. Sheeba had made it very clear from the onset that she had nothing to offer other than friendship, but to Abhishek that was all what he wanted—partnering her to success. They would discuss about his marriage, but he would break off the discussion stating how impossible it would be for him to love someone else. Love is interesting. At least it does make conversations short.

Sheeba could very well have settled with Abhishek. He was wealthy, loved her truly and had good business acumen, but the past always has the tendency to smother the future if you allow it to. Sheeba could not reconcile the rejection she faced from him years ago. It still rankles. True, he had more than made up for it. However, the scar remained. Moreover, Jamie was still a lingering thought.

This is the man who has helped her build her empire. Otherwise, she would still have inhabited some tacky apartment tucked away in some backyard of the city. He had promised support. He gave more—much much more.

Sheeba had all the opportunity to marry Abhishek. He had everything a woman would want. He also believed in the best and could spend as much to own it. Jamie could not afford so much. In fact, Jamie was never in the league of Abhishek. But for Sheeba that could never be the reason to leave someone. Wealth attracted her as long as it was earned. She was attuned to the struggle. The roadside tea attracted her more than that of The Taj, though she was equal at ease with both.

Love is an illusion. It creates a facade of balance—only to topple the unsuspecting. Madz would keep advising her about the non-existence of a perfect marriage. She would tell her to get married to someone her heart yearned for; someone she would love to wake up with, giggle with and take a shower with; and someone who can be a partner in her daily chores—who will be a friend first and much later, a husband. Sheeba did find all these in Jamie. She was the benchmark of a partner, and so was Abhishek too. As mentioned earlier, they both were Librans and blindly fond of Sheeba.

It was now turning into a classic case of whom to listen. The brain suggested Abhishek—the rich kid—and lead a lavish life without the bother of sustenance, but her heart was stuck somewhere very far. It was in a world of its own, and it preferred that way.

Sheeba wanted to be on her own, to create her own identity and to manufacture—for want of a better word—her own dreams and live it. She wanted the very best for Shanaya—her angel. Abhishek would treat Shanaya like his own daughter. Her every want—and there were almost none—would be met immediately. They would discuss matters like grown-ups, with Shanaya correcting Abhishek's diction along the way. It was fun to have them both together. Sheeba knew Abhishek would make a cool step dad. However, the idea of having one frightened her. The past would again return to haunt her.

Shanaya is a possessive child—a trait she inherited from her parents. She was also way intelligent beyond her eleven years. She knew Sheeba at times would contemplate marrying Abhishek and her advice was being sought, for which Shanaya would suggest her to get back to her husband, if she at all wanted one, "Abhi uncle is good, but not a husband, mom. You have me, Hunter and Jamie for everything else. If you really need one, get back to your own." Children enlighten you. They always do.

It's been nine years that they have been separated, but the process of divorce has been excruciatingly slow. Every time they wanted to wrap it up and something else would come up.

Edward did call up the other day asking her to expedite the proceedings. Sheeba was in no hurry though. She not only loved her Irish surname but also feared Shanaya would take it otherwise. She was waiting for Shanaya to enter teenage, and probably then she would be able to understand the nuances of life better. Sheeba really did not want to burn her fingers again.

Shanaya would ask Sheeba to carry on living with Jamie, unknowing to the kind of relationship they shared. Sheeba worried about the day when Shanaya would actually get to know the reality, and all hell would break loose.

That night Sheeba—like all other nights—sat for her prayers before hitting the sack. She prayed for Edward, Jamie and Abhishek—people who have shaped her and made her ready to face life. They were very important cogs in her wheel.

A little voice sprang up from within.

"Sheeba, the reason I have removed these people from your life has got nothing to do with you. I have simply moved them away, for their purpose in your life has been fulfilled. I want to take you to the next level and all I want you to is grow and not have people create hindrances for you. Let them go and you keep moving, my child."

That night, Sheeba slept like a small child after so many years.

Chapter 10

Mornings are always rush hour. It's a war—trenches everywhere. It's a battle every woman in the world fights, and wins. Along the rush, Sheeba catches a glimpse of herself—the dishevelled hair and the kohl-lined eye. It was a leftover from the last night's party. The doorbell rings. It is her new rose gold iPhone 6S—agift to herself.

The day was spent shopping all by herself—checking into a spa and purchasing some expensive distractions from the MAC store, a Versace her and an Issey Miyake there. She had lunch at an exclusive fine dining and returned home fulfilled.

Other than these infrequent indulgences, it is only work for Sheeba. Shanaya and Hunter take up most of her waking hours too. She loves the place she has created for herself with life. They seem to be at ease with each other. Sheeba has had her fill with men, sex, booze, drugs and parties. She is done with the recklessness. She is now more into detoxification. Yoga helps her do that. It's more the mind she needs to calm than the body. She has a personal trainer who attends her once a week. One of the benefits of heartbreak has been the reduction in her weight, though she does not suggest it be done this way. But anything can make you fit into your loving clothes.

She does keep looking into her phone to check for messages from Jamie. Rarely there are messages. Then, she drowns herself in work. She hopes to earn good enough money to fulfil her dreams and needs and also for those who she loves and takes care of. Andrew and Mohsin do bump into her at times, but they are so insignificant to her now that she cannot be bothered of them anymore.

Edward and Sheeba have finally moved towards their divorce. It will take some more time to finally settle this. They still do argue and fret over Shanaya and her upbringing—loving parents that they both are. The little angel would at time rue the fact that how much she misses a family. Sheeba would make her understand how much her daddy and mommy loved her. But to the impressionable mind of a child a separation is a catastrophe and no amount of cajoling can better that. Somewhere deep within Sheeba too misses a husband—a person who could be her sounding board. She knows that will never be happening again. There is a sense of anxiety of being all alone and taking on the world.

Sheeba knows her marriage is over. She does try to prick the exact reasons for it, but she does not remember. Probably there were too many. She does not blame Edward for anything. It's time to move ahead. It's just damn too late to look back.

Abhi is still there—as the mentor and the last resort. They still bond over frivolities. Jamie is there too. They meet up at times. They discuss life over lunch or dinner. Sometimes they catch up for a movie too. They still are long-lost friends, but the lovers in them have set sail long ago.

Love is an emotional verb. It's a feeling you need to work upon. It just does not end with sweet words but backed by strong actions. The reason why Sheeba's relationship failed was because of this. They all lacked affirmative actions—even Sheeba lacked. She misses a relationship, but then life is meant to be stark and void. It needs action to fill it up.

She is lost in her thought when her assistant brings over a piping hot cup of coffee. The pain suddenly fizzles, and the mind alerts her to the day ahead. It's another day in paradise, and Sheeba loves it that way.

This is the final chapter of Sheeba's journey thus far. Had she written earlier, we would have missed all the new characters in her life. They made Sheeba the person she is—contoured her future with the silhouettes of experience. This is the closure she wanted—a healing she was so frantically been searching for.

She does carry a notepad everywhere to jot down her thoughts and incorporate it into her tale. It does come to her in the most obscure of places. But isn't life all about weirdness?

Sheeba's journey could be anyone's. The billions teeming on the face of this planet have similar tales to tell. We are all unique in our own juxtapositions—fighting our fears commendably. Life and love have been great partners but necessarily should never be mixed. They say that if you wish to live, don't love and if you want to love, then die every day.

Probably that's how it's meant to be. But don't we love a good love story where we all live? Happiness and sadness depend on one's a state of mind. It's a prism through which you engage yourself, and that's so very important—engaging oneself. Sheeba is currently on her journey discovering just that—herself!

A note from the author

Hope you guys enjoyed reading this journey of a woman and why she falls in love with a lesbian. Nothing is ever planned by you. You are destined to the path you walk on, and some are circumstantial.

While writing this book, I have tried to stay clear of any affiliations and influence. I have tried to be as truthful as possible and that is to say that I have said it all. I wanted this to be my story in the same manner I have experienced the life.

It is my path and my journey, though I am yet to fathom my destination. Maybe in the future when I am nearing one, I would indulge in another tale.

Regards,

Sheeba

Chapter 11

A little message to all my characters!

To my bong cute angel who I did not marry, but wish I could…

My Dearest Abhi,

I hope you fall in love with someone who always calls you back and never lets you fall asleep unwanted. I hope you fall in love with someone who holds your hands during the scary parts of horror movies and burns cookies with you, while you both are busy dancing around the kitchen. I hope you fall in love with someone who tickles you and makes you laugh on hard days and easy ones too. But beyond all that I hope you will fall in love with someone who will never take you for granted or leave you; someone who will stand by you when you're wrong and when you're right; someone who has seen your worst and loves you still; and someone who kisses you in the rain and hugs you when you're cold and wouldn't have it any other way.

Sorry for all the times I took you and your love for granted. Please know you will always occupy a very special place in my heart forever—no matter where we are!

To My Ex-Husband Edward,

A doting father—in fact the very best—I cannot describe in words. The best human being I have ever come across.

We just didn't make it because destiny had other plans. You are the most special person in my life because you gave me Shanaya—my most precious gift of creation. I wish you only happiness, peace and Love.

Madhumita (Madz)

She's the woman who believes that what comes around goes around—the eternal pragmatist and the one who won't give up on you. She's the woman, so unlike the rest. You are the one who would love to be loved—the one who looks bloody strong but is also the reason for your weakness. You are the one—Madz—who will pick herself up every time she fell.

Akira

Be the sister that you always are, thank you for being there for me. I will always love you; you are more of my best friend than a sister.

Dev (Editor)

A friend—whom I met on the social network—is a thorough gentleman, who willingly helped me through editing this book. I will always be grateful to you.

Shanaya

If this book gets published, this will be your fourteenth birthday gift. You will live my journey through this book. All your questions and confusions are bound to vanish. I do not know if you would hate me or love me, but all I want for you is to know who your real mother is.

You will always be the most precious gift of mine. I will carry you in my heart until I die—just like the way I carried you in my womb. Remember that you will be the first love of your mother's—no matter who comes in her life. You are the reason I breathe. I cannot measure how much I love you.

I don't know if I love you more than dad does or grandma does, but I can assure you that I love you. You will certainly know a mother's love once you become a mother yourself.

As I have always told you, respect your father. It is because of him I have you. Always love your parents.

My Precious Jamie,

You have perennially complained that I was never in love with you as much as you were. True, you have loved me selflessly, but I had already built a wall around me, so that no one or nothing could hurt me anymore.

My journey with you has been one of a kind—most exclusive. It is still my favourite love story. Today I admit to the world that I have loved you most among all. I wish ours did not ever end. Today I do feel the distance that I have bridged between us. I will willingly take all the blame if this did not work out. Living and reliving our lives again has been quite a struggle. You have tried your best to keep me, but I guess it required a harder push. Today we live like roommates, friends and soulmates. There is an easy relationship, but you care less for love which is fully understandable.

Your perception of our relationship has changed. You want a committed relationship, and you bicker all the time that I don't give you enough time and you want an understanding and a loving girlfriend.

My only wish for you is that you find the shining star you're searching for.

One day someone will walk into your life and bring all of the beauty you never saw in yourself back to the surface again. It won't seem forced. It won't feel like a hidden agenda. You actually won't even notice how easy your walls come down until after the fact.

Special people have means of reaching places inside of you that you normally wouldn't allow people into. They give you reassurance they aren't out to hurt you. And when bad times do arise, they end up being the first to wipe your tears or the last person standing up to help you fight your fears.

One day a person like this will definitely walk into your life and make you feel like being in love is actually pretty easy. And "easy love" is just the best love you can have.

Hunter

My Life,

I know you're my pet, but I consider you my son. I love you as much as I love Shanaya. You are the son I always wanted and desired. The day you jumped into my lap and looked at me with those puppy eyes I knew we were meant to share the mother–son bonding. I am sure someday somebody will read this out to you and you would understand every single thing I've penned down—just like the way you understood me so well.

You alone have taught me to love selflessly without any conditions. The long nights I kept awake, you'd be awake with me—caressing my forehead with your furry paws and tail. I shudder at the thought you would just stay with me for fifteen odd years and I get sleepless again. I cannot imagine my life without you.

You know the best thing I love about you is when you wake me up with your wet fur and pull my blankets off—telling me to wake up and get ready for work. It would be a shame if I considered you a human. I hope you do remember when I threatened my family members to stop visiting me if they did not accept you as my son and the times when my friends would call and say, "Please lock your dog up"—how I would get hysterical and ask them not to come? I remember all of that too. Since the time you arrived, I knew I did not need anyone but you. Even Shanaya was forced to like you and play with you, and see how Shanaya cannot stay away from you now. You have turned her into your best friend.

I love the way you stare at me with your dark brown eyes—especially when you tilt your head to one side, when I talk lovingly to you. I am sorry for beating you with the newspaper for leaving me and running away from home. I did it only because I panicked how I'd survive without you. I love cleaning your dirt, after you mess up the whole house. I remember how I would keep awake for Shanaya when she was unwell, and I would do it for you too. I would love to do it for another hundred years. I promise to give you the best in life.

I promise to take you wherever I go except if it's hell.

I will never put you in a shelter and leave.

I will never let you starve. I will never hurt you.

I will never desert you when you get old, nor will I leave you when you go blind. If that comes, I will be there to hold you because I love you and you are my family and home.

Your mommy,

Sheeba